CONTENTS

ILLUSTRATIONS

translated by
John Porter

with drawings by
Andy Selwood

Copyright © 1994 John Porter
and Andy Selwood.
Llanerch Publishers, Felinfach.
ISBN 1 897853 13 0

Bandamanna saga
Power and Responsibility

The use and abuse of power is a central issue in many of the Icelandic family sagas. This concern is likely to reflect the political conditions of the thirteenth century, when the narratives were composed, rather than those of the tenth and eleventh centuries, in which the events themselves are set.

In *Bandamanna saga,* old Ofeig's deeply sarcastic question to his son: 'How could a fault be found in the prosecution of a rich man like you?' is a withering comment on the way in which men of established wealth and power could protect their own interests through manipulation of the legal process. The chieftains who form a band to oppose Odd, do so from motives of avarice and envy, not in order to restore justice to an innocent victim. The author does not suggest that the corruption of the power system can be reformed from within the ranks of the chieftains themselves, and so it is an outsider, the impoverished but wily Ofeig, who becomes the unlikely hero of the saga's moral and political dimension.

In fighting to save his son's case against Ospak for the killing of Vali, he resorts to bribery of the judges as a means of persuading them to a proper understanding of the spirit of the oaths of their office. As he says to his son: 'Money makes many a man's eye squint,' and the scene in which he dangles the fat purse in and out of their view while talking of the principles of truth and justice provides one of the blackest pieces of comedy in saga literature.

In defending the consequences of his own illegality, and protecting Odd from the combined power of the greedy band, he finds himself opposing his own chieftain, Styrmir. With a combination of flattery and threat, cajolery and bluff and brilliant opportunism, he succeeds in dividing the enemy and getting the charges dropped. This opens the way for the two great show-downs, in which the personal and social failings of the individual members of the band are exposed to public ridicule, and their petty ambitions defeated. If meanness, malice, greed, pride, incompetence, dishonesty and cowardice are the ruling characteristics of those who wield power, it is ironically apt that the band is betrayed from within by its own lack of integrity.

Enclosing the central, public, historical
theme is the private and psychological
issue of the relationship between father
and son. Odd's commercial success has
been achieved through individual enterprise
in a state of deep but unexplained
alienation from his father. Wealth has
enabled him to buy power, but it has not
brought him the shrewdness or knowledge
necessary to maintain it under pressure.
His errors of judgement with the dubious
Ospak, whose ambitions are so similar to
his own, ultimately prove fatal to his only
close friend. His inadequacy at law and his
inability to appreciate the seriousness of
the opposition threaten all he has accomplished. When he accepts his father's
assistance, he does so grudgingly and on
cash-in-hand terms, the only ones which
the merchant trader seems to understand.

Yet it is on behalf of this naive and
colourless son that Ofeig gains his triumph
at the assembly. With the defeat of the
band, filial love and friendship are re-
stored, and with his whirlwind trip to the
Orkneys for wedding supplies, Odd
demonstrates a renewal of the luck which
brought him material success. Odd's fresh

7

liaison with Gellir, and his generosity to Egil seem the basis of a promising future, in which the young chieftain might mature into a man worthy of both wealth and power.

John Porter, 1993.

Chapter 1

There was a man called Ofeig,
who lived in the west of Iceland in
Midfjord at a farm called Reykir.
He was the son of Skidi, and his
mother's name was Gunnlaug. Her
mother was Jarngerd, who was the
daughter of Ofeig Jarngerdarson from
Skord in the north. Ofeig was married, and his wife's name was
Thorgerd. Her father's name was
Vali, and she came from a prominent
family and was a clever and distin-
guished woman. Ofeig was a very
wise man and full of shrewd advice.
In all he did he showed great abil-
ity, but he was not too well off for
money. He owned a good deal of
land, but less in the way of ready
assets. He didn't stint anyone of his
food, but had a hard struggle to pro-
vide household necessities. He was
a follower of the chieftain Styrmir
from Asgeirs River, who was held to

be the most important chieftain there at that time.

Ofeig and his wife had a son named Odd. He was a good-looking man and showed promise at an early age. His father did not show him much affection. Odd was not keen on work.

There was a man called Vali who was brought up in Ofeig's home. He was a good-looking and popular man.

Odd grew up at home with his father until he was twelve years old. Ofeig behaved coolly towards him most of the time and had little love for him. Rumour had it that no-one in the district was more capable than Odd.

One day Odd got talking with his father and asked him for money.

"I want to get away from here," he said. "The way things are, you have no respect for me, and I am no

Odd leaving Ofeig's house.

12

use to you in your affairs."

"What I'll give you won't be any less than what you deserve," replied Ofeig, "in fact I'll make it almost exactly that, and then you'll see what good it will do you."

Odd said he could hardly support himself on that, and their talk ended.

The next day Odd took down from the wall a full set of fishing gear and six yards of woollen cloth. Then he went away without telling anyone. He went out to Vatnsnes and joined up with some fishermen. From them he got the things he needed most, on loan and on credit. And when they saw that he was from a good family and was popular, then they risked trusting him. He bought everything on credit and stayed fishing with them for a time. It is said that the crew Odd was with had the best luck with the fish. He was there for three years, and by

then he had done so well that not
only had he paid back everyone what
he owed, but had laid up some cap-
ital as well. He never went to see
his father, and both of them acted as
if the other were no concern of his.
Odd was well-liked by his compan-
ions.

In due course he made a business out of ferrying goods north to
the farms along the Hornstrand coast,
and bought a share in a ferry-boat
and made a living out of it. He soon
began to make money, and bought the
boat outright, and went on plying
between Midfjord and Hornstrand for
a few summers. Now he began to
get quite rich.

Eventually he grew tired of this
occupation. He bought a share in a
merchant ship and went abroad on
trading journeys for a while. Again
he handled this with skill and success, and again he got money and a
good name from it. He pressed

ahead with this work until he owned the ship outright, and most of the freight too. He made trading journeys and became a very rich and famous man. He often stayed with chieftains and men of high rank abroad, and was well thought of wherever he went. He became so rich that he had two ships out trading. It was said that there was no sea merchant as wealthy as Odd at that time. He was also luckier than other men with his voyages. He never made a landfall north of Eyjafjord or west of Hrutafjord.

Chapter 2

The story goes that one summer Odd put in to Bordeyr in Hrutafjord, planning to stay in Iceland over the winter. His friends asked him to settle down there, so he fell in with their wishes and bought some land in Midfjord at a place called Mel. He set up a great household there and lived in grand style on his farm, and it is said that this venture was thought no less successful than his trading voyages were before. There was now no man as famous as Odd in the northern districts. He used his money better than most other men, and was helpful to neighbours who needed him in times of difficulty. But he never provided any comfort for his father. He laid up his ship in Hrutafjord. It was said that no-one in Iceland was as

Odd's farm at Mel.

wealthy as Odd; in fact people said that he had no less money than the three richest men put together. He had wealth of every kind -- gold and silver, land and livestock. His kinsman Vali was always with him, whether he was at home in Iceland or abroad. Odd lived at home on his farm in great honour, as was said before.

There was a man named Glum. He lived at Skridnesenni, between Bitra and Kollafjord. He had a wife named Thordis, who was the daughter of Asmund greyhair, Grettir's father. Their son was called Ospak. He was a big, strong man, hard to get along with and quarrelsome. In his young days he worked at ferrying goods from the Hornstrand coast to the northern districts. He was a capable man, and grew up physically powerful. One summer he came to

Midfjord and sold his share of the business. And one day he got himself a horse and rode up to Mel and found Odd. They exchanged greetings and asked each other the general news.

Ospak said, "The thing is, Odd, that you have a good reputation for business; people praise you highly, and everyone in your household thinks himself well-placed. Now I hope it will turn out like that for me; I want to move up here with you."

Odd replied, "People don't praise you highly, and you are not well-liked. You've got a crafty kind of look in your eyes, just like the rest of your family."

"Judge that for yourself," said Ospak, "and not by hearsay, since not many men get a better name than they deserve. I'm not asking you for any gifts. I'd like to live under your roof, but I'll find my own food, and then let's see how you take to the idea."

Odd replied, "You and your kinsmen are powerful, and hard to quell if you feel like making enemies, but since you urge me so hard to take you in, we can take a chance on it for one winter."

Ospak accepted gratefully, and went to Mel with his belongings in the autumn, and soon devoted himself to Odd, busied himself around the farm and did the work of two men. Odd was well pleased with him.

The season passed by. When spring came, Odd said he thought it would be better if Ospak moved into the farmhouse. Ospak was happy about it. He was busy about the farm, and everything was going well.

Everyone thought that Ospak was proving himself well, and he was popular, too. The farm was now flourishing, and Odd's fortunes were thought to be at a supreme pitch.

The crowning of his honour seemed to lack only one thing, which was that he had no chieftainship. At that time it was common for men to establish new chieftainships, or to buy them, and that is what Odd did. Followers quickly flocked to him; everyone was eager to have him for a leader. And now things were quiet for a while.

Chapter 3

Odd was well pleased with Ospak, and let him have his own way with most of the farm business. He worked hard and for long hours, and was invaluable on the estate. The winter passed and Odd was more pleased than ever with Ospak, because now he took on even more. In the autumn he gathered in the sheep from the fells, and it was a successful round-up, with not a single sheep missing. Winter gave way to spring. Odd announced that he was planning to go abroad in the summer, and said that his kinsman Vali was to be in charge of the farm. Vali replied, "It so happens, kinsman, that I've had no practice at that, and I would rather look after our goods and cargo." Then Odd turned to Ospak, and asked him to take over the farm.

"That's more than I could handle alone," said Ospak, "though everything goes quite well when you are here."

Odd pressed him, but Ospak refused, though he was itching to accept. And in the end he told Odd to have his own way, on condition that he promised him his protection and goodwill. Odd told him to manage his property so as to get the greatest honour and popularity from it, and said he knew that no-one else was better able or willing to look after his possessions. Ospak said it was entirely Odd's decision, and they left it at that.

Odd made his ship ready and had the cargo brought aboard. The news got round and was much discussed. Odd did not need long to get ready. Vali was travelling with

24

him. When he was ready to sail, his men went with him to the ship. Ospak stayed with him for longer than the others; they had a lot to discuss. When they had almost reached the ship, Odd said, "There's just one thing which has not been settled."

"What's that," said Ospak.

"No arrangements have been made about my chieftaincy," said Odd, "and I want you to take charge of it."

"That's senseless," said Ospak. "I'm not capable of it. I've already taken on more than I'm likely to be able to handle or cope with properly. No-one is better cut out for this than your father. He is well-versed in law, and a very wise man."

Odd said he would not hand it over to his father. "I want you to take it."

Ospak refused, though in fact he really wanted it. Odd said he would be angry if he did not take it, and when they parted Ospak took over the chieftaincy. Then Odd went abroad, and as usual he had a successful journey.

Ospak went home, and there was a lot of talk about what had happened. People thought that Odd had put a lot of power into this man's hands.

Ospak rode to the Assembly in the summer with a band of men, and conducted things well and efficiently. He was able to cope well with all his legal obligations, and he rode away from the Assembly with honour. He supported his men's interests vigorously, so that none of them suffered any loss, and they were not subject to much provocation. He was kind and open-handed to all his neighbours. The generosity and hospitality of the household seemed no less than before. The skilled management of the farm did not flag, and affairs went well. Summer passed by. Ospak rode to the autumn Assembly and hallowed it, and towards the end of autumn he went up to the fells with the men to gather in the sheep. It was a good round-up; the search was thorough, and not a single sheep of either his or Odd's was missing.

Chapter 4

In the autumn Ospak happened to go north into Vididal to Svolustadir, where a woman called Svala lived. He was well entertained there. She was a young woman, and good-looking. She spoke with Ospak, and asked him to look after her affairs – "I've heard that you are a skilful farm manager." He was pleased at this, and they had a long talk. They took a great liking to each other, and exchanged amorous looks. Eventually he asked her who was responsible for arranging her marriage.

"The nearest of my kinsmen who amounts to anything," she said, "is Thorarin the Wise, the chieftain of the Langadal men."

So Ospak rode to see Thorarin, and got a rather cool welcome. He broached the purpose of his visit, and asked to marry Svala.

"I don't know that I'm keen to have you for a kinsman," said Thorarin. "There's a lot of talk about the way you behave. I can see that one can't juggle around with men like you; either I've got to deprive her of her farm and have her come to live here, or else the two of you will do as you please. So I'll have no part of it, but I won't give my consent."

After that Ospak went away and came back to Svolustadir and told Svala what had happened. So they arranged their marriage, and she herself betrothed herself to him, and went with him to Mel. But they kept the farm at Svolustadir and put tenants in there to look after it. Ospak stayed at Mel now, and kept up the affluent style of life in the farm. Even so, he was thought to be a very domineering man.

Winter passed, and during the summer Odd arrived in Hrutafjord; yet again he had been financially and personally successful. He came home to Mel and looked over his property; it seemed to have been well cared for, and he was pleased. Summer wore on. One day Odd put it to Ospak that it would be a good idea for him to take back his chieftaincy

"Yes," said Ospak, "that's the thing I was least eager to shoulder and least suited for, and I'm quite ready to return it, but I think it's the usual practice to do it either at the autumn Assembly or the district Assembly."

"That's quite possibly the case," said Odd.

So summer passed on towards the autumn Assembly, and on the morning of the Assembly, when Odd

woke up, he looked around and could not see anyone in the hall. He had slept long and soundly. He jumped up, and realised that the hall was quite deserted. He thought this strange, but didn't say much. He and a handful of men made ready and rode to the Assembly. When they arrived a lot of people were there, but they were almost ready to go home again, and the Assembly had been hallowed. Odd was amazed and thought the whole thing extraordinary. People returned home, and a few days passed by.

One day Odd was sitting at table, with Ospak facing him. Suddenly Odd jumped up from the table and straight at Ospak with a raised axe in his hand, and told him to hand over the chieftaincy.

"No need to chase it so fiercely," said Ospak. "You can have the chieftaincy whenever you want it; I didn't realise you were serious about taking it back." Then he stretched out his hand and consigned the chieftaincy to Odd. Things were quiet for a while, and from this time relations cooled between Odd and Ospak. Ospak was rather fierce to deal with. People suspected he had planned to keep the chieftaincy for himself and not return it to Odd if he could have prevented it being forced away from him. Nothing got done on the farm now; Odd didn't call on him to do anything, nor did they speak to each other. One day Ospak made ready to leave. Odd acted as if he knew nothing of it, and so they parted without even a greeting. Ospak went to his farm at Svolustadir. Odd acted as if nothing had happened. All was quiet for a time.

It is said that in the autumn the men went to the fells, and compared with previous occasions there was a very great difference in the number of Odd's sheep which were rounded up. At the autumn gathering, he was short of the forty best wethers in his flock. The search went on far and wide around the fells and moors, but they were not found. This was thought to be very strange, for Odd was considered luckier with his sheep than other men. So extensive was the search, that they were hunted both locally and in other districts, but nothing came of it. In time the matter was dropped, though there was a lot of talk about what was behind it.

Odd was not cheerful during the winter. His kinsman Vali asked him why he was gloomy -- "does the disappearance of the sheep mean so

much to you? You're not much of a
man if a thing like that upsets
you."

"The disappearance of the sheep
doesn't upset me," replied Odd.
"What bothers me more is that I
don't know who stole them."

"Are you sure that is what really happened to them?" asked Vali,
"and if so, who is your first suspect?"

"I won't hide the fact that I
think Ospak stole them," said Odd.

"Your friendship is not what it
was when you gave him charge of all
your possessions," said Vali.

Odd said that had been a co-
lossal blunder, but it had turned out
better than expected.

"A lot of people said it was
strange," said Vali. "Now I don't
want you to be so hasty in accusing
him; that way there's a risk of peo-

ple saying it's slander. We'll make a bargain that you shall let me decide how to go about it, and I shall find out the truth."

They agreed on this.

Vali made ready for a journey, and took his merchandise with him. He rode out to Vatnsdal and Langadal and sold his goods. He was well-liked and obliging. He went on his way until he came to Svolustadir, where he was well entertained. Ospak was very cheerful. Vali got ready to leave in the morning. Ospak went with him out of the yard and asked a lot of questions about Odd. Vali said his affairs were going well. Ospak spoke well of him and called him a very generous man. "Has he had any losses this autumn?"

Vali said he had.

"What are people saying about

the missing sheep?" asked Ospak. "Odd has always been lucky with his sheep up to now."

"There's no single opinion," said Vali. "Some think there was a man's hand in it."

"That's unthinkable," said Ospak. "Not many people get up to tricks like that."

"There it is," said Vali.

"What is Odd's guess?" asked Ospak.

"He doesn't say much about it," said Vali, "but other people can't stop talking about what's behind it."

"That's natural," said Ospak.

"The fact is," said Vali, "since we're talking about it, that some men are saying it's not unlikely that you're to blame. They connect the facts that you and Odd parted on bad terms and that the sheep went missing not long after."

"I didn't expect you to talk like that," replied Ospak, "and if we were not such friends I would take a heavy revenge for this."

"You've no need to hide it or react so violently," said Vali. "You can't get out of it. I've looked over your farm, and I see that you have more things than you're likely to have come by honestly."

"It can't be proved," said Ospak. "I don't know what our enemies are saying, if friends are talking like this."

"What I say to you in private is not said out of enmity," said Vali. "Now if you do as I wish, and confess to me, then you'll get off lightly, because I'll arrange things that way. I have sold my goods far and wide around the district; I will say that you have taken the money on loan and bought meat and other things

with it. No one will doubt me. I'll
see to it that you get no shame out of
this if you follow my advice."

Ospak said he would not confess
to it.

"Then it will be the worse for
you," said Vali, "and it will be your
own fault."

After that they parted and Vali
went home. Odd asked what he had
found out about the missing sheep.
Vali didn't have much to say about
it.

"There's no need to hide the fact
that Ospak stole them," said Odd,
"because you'ld be only too glad to
speak up for him if you could."

Things were quiet during the
winter. When spring came and the
summoning days arrived, Odd rode
out with twenty men until they had
almost reached the farm at Svolustadir.

Then Vali said to Odd, "Now you must let your horses graze, and I will ride to the farm to find Ospak, and find out if he wants to arrange a settlement, in which case the matter need go no further."

They did so, and Vali rode to the farm. There was no-one outside. The door was open. Vali went in. It was dark inside the house. Without any warning someone jumped up from the side-dais and struck Vali between the shoulders, so that he fell to the ground.

"Save yourself, you wretch," said Vali, "because Odd is not far off and he means to kill you. Send your wife to him, and have her say that we've come to terms and that you've confessed, and that I've gone further up the valley to collect a debt."

"This is a disaster," said Ospak. "I meant it for Odd, not you."

Svala found Odd and said that Ospak and Vali had come to terms – "and Vali said you were to turn back." Odd believed her, and rode home. Vali died, and his body was brought to Mel. Odd thought it was a monstrous act. He lost a lot of face by it, and people thought it was a terrible blunder. Ospak disappeared, and no-one knew what had become of him.

Ospak's killing of Vali.

Chapter 5

Now the story goes that Odd got ready to prosecute this case at the Assembly, and cited nine local farmers as witnesses. One of them happened to die, and Odd cited another in his place. Then people travelled to the Assembly, and it was uneventful until the courts sat. When the courts went into session, Odd pleaded his case for manslaughter, and it went smoothly. Then the defence was called.

Not far from the court, the chieftains Styrmir and Thorarin were sitting with their followers. Styrmir said to Thorarin, "Now the defence has been called in the manslaughter case; are you going to reply to it?"

"I'm not going to meddle in that one," replied Thorarin, "for it seems to me that Odd has reason enough to sue for the killing of a man like Vali, and in my opinion the accused man is a rogue."

"Yes," said Styrmir, "it's true he's no good, yet you do have a certain duty to him."

"I couldn't care less," said Thorarin.

"You have to take into account that you'll face a lot of difficult problems if he's convicted," said Styrmir, "and I think it's worth looking in to, so let's work out a plan, because we can both see a loophole in the case."

"I saw it long ago," said Thorarin, "but I don't like the idea of throwing up obstacles."

"But you're the one who'll be most affected," said Styrmir, "and people will say you've acted shabbily if the case is carried through, when the defence is clear as day. And it's

46

also a fact that it would be just as well if Odd found out he's not the only man who counts. He tramples us all underfoot, and our followers, so that his name is the only one you hear. It wouldn't hurt to let him know his limits as a lawyer."

"Have it your own way, then," said Thorarin, "and I'll back you up. But I don't like the smell of it, and it will turn out for the worse."

"Don't worry about that," said Styrmir. He jumped up and went to the court, and asked how the lawsuits were going. They told him.

"It so happens, Odd, that a fault has been found in your case," said Styrmir. "You prepared it wrongly. You cited ten neighbours as witnesses at your domicile, and that's not in accord with the law. It should have been done here at the Assembly, and not in your own district. Either withdraw from the court now, and leave things as they stand, or we shall put forward the defence."

Odd was silent, and thought the matter over. He realised it was true, and left the court with his followers and went back to his booth. When he entered the passage between his booth and the next, there was a man coming towards him. He was an old man. He was wearing a black sleeved cape which was falling to pieces; it had only one sleeve, and that was twisted round to the back. In his hand he had a long staff with a spike in it. He was wearing a long hood; beneath it the eyes were wide open. He was banging the staff down on the ground and walking along with a stoop. It was old Ofeig, his father.

"You're soon back from the

A. GREENWOOD © 93

court," he said. "You've got more than one talent if all your affairs wind up so smoothly and quickly. Was that Ospak found guilty?"

"No," said Odd, "he was not found guilty."

"It's not fair for a chieftain to make fun of an old man like me," said Ofeig. "Why wasn't he found guilty? Wasn't he guilty of the charge?"

"Of course he was," said Odd.

"What's up then?" said Ofeig. "I would have thought the charge would stick! He was the one who killed Vali, wasn't he?"

"No-one's denying it," said Odd.

"Then why wasn't he found guilty," said Ofeig.

"There was a fault found in the case, and it fell through," said Odd.

"How could a fault be found in

the prosecution of a rich man like you?" said Ofeig.

"They said the local preparations were wrong," said Odd.

"That can't be true if you were handling it," said Ofeig, "but it could be true that you're better at money-grubbing and travelling abroad than at steering lawsuits along skilfully. But I can hardly believe you're telling me the truth."

"I don't care if you believe me or not," said Odd.

"That may be so," said Ofeig, "but I knew as soon as you left home that the case had been wrongly prepared, but you thought you were good enough on your own, and wouldn't ask anyone for help. And now you'll have to be good enough on your own in defeat. No doubt you'll do all right out of it; that's always the way with people who think everyone else inferior."

"Even so, it's obvious that you will be no help," said Odd.

"There's only one thing that can help your case now," said Ofeig, "and that's if you use me. But how tight-fisted would you be now, if someone were to put the case right?"

"I wouldn't be tight-fisted at all, if someone would take up the case," said Odd.

"Then let these old hands of mine feel the weight of a fat purse," said Ofeig. "Money makes many a man's eye squint."

Odd gave him a big purse of money. Then Ofeig asked, "was the defence plea actually put forward, or not?"

"We left the court beforehand," said Odd.

"Our one advantage is in what

you did in ignorance," said Ofeig.

So they parted, and Odd went back to his booth.

Chapter 6

Now the story goes that old Ofeig went up on the plain to the courts. He came to the Northerners' court, and asked how the cases were going. He was told that some had already been judged, and that others were ready for summing-up.

"What's happening in the case of my son, Odd?" he asked. "Is it finished yet?"

"As finished as it will ever be," they said.

"Was Ospak found guilty?" asked Ofeig.

"No," they said, "he was not."

"What was the reason?" asked Ofeig.

"A fault was found in the case," they said; "it was wrongly prepared."

"I see," said Ofeig. "Will you

allow me to enter the court?"

They agreed, and he went into the court-ring, and sat down.

"Has the case of my son, Odd, been judged?" asked Ofeig.

"As judged as it ever will be," they said.

"Why is that?" asked Ofeig." "Was something wrong with the accusation against Ospak? Did he not kill Vali without cause? Was it not an open and shut case?"

"A fault was found in the case, and it fell through," they said.

"What kind of fault was that?" asked Ofeig.

They told him.

"Indeed," said Ofeig, "and do you think it at all just to pay attention to such trifles, yet to acquit this rogue, this thief, this killer? Aren't you taking on a great responsibility in thwarting the course of justice by acquitting a man who deserves death?"

They said that they did not think it just, but that it was what the law demanded.

That may be so," said Ofeig. "Did you swear the oath?"

"Of course," they said.

"Of course, you had to," he said, "and what was the form of words you spoke? Was it not like this, that you would judge 'as you knew to be most true, most just, and most lawful'? That's what you must have sworn."

They said that was so.

Then Ofeig said, "But what is more true, or more just, than to find a rogue guilty, and able to be killed with impunity, and cut off from all help, when he has been duly found guilty of theft and of killing Vali, an innocent man? But the third clause of the oath would have to be twisted a bit. Think it over, though; which carries greater weight, the two clauses concerning truth and justice, or the one that concerns the letter of the law? Then you will realise what is obvious, because you will surely be able to see that it is a very serious thing to acquit a man who deserves to die, when you've just sworn an oath that you would judge as you knew to be most just. So you can see that this will turn out badly for you, and you can scarcely escape this grave responsibility."

Every so often Ofeig lowered the purse from beneath his cloak, and then drew it up again. He watched their eyes straying to the purse. Then he said to them, "It would be more advisable to make a just and true judgement, as you have sworn to do, and in return to gain the thanks and appreciation of wise and just men."

Then he took the purse and poured out the silver and counted it in front of them.

"Now I want to do you a friendly turn," he said, "and to show you that I'm more concerned for you in this matter than for myself; and I'm doing this because some of you are my friends, and some my kinsmen, but you all have to look after your own interests. I will give an ounce of silver to each man who sits in the court, and half a mark to those who are summing up the case. Then you'll have the money as well as having discharged your responsibilities, and you will not have broken your oaths, which is the most important thing."

They thought it over, and found there was some truth in his argument, feeling especially the seriousness of breaking the oath, and they chose to accept Ofeig's offer. Then Odd was sent for immediately, and he came. By then the chieftains had gone back to their booths. The case was re-opened straight away, and Ospak was found guilty, and then witnesses for the final judgement were named. When this had been done, everyone returned to their booths.

No news of this spread during the night. At the Law Rock in the morning Odd stood up and said in a loud voice, "Here in the Northerners' court last night a man named Ospak was made an outlaw for the manslaughter of Vali. These are the signs by which the outlaw may be recognised: he is a tall, tough-looking man; he has brown hair and a big-boned face, black brows, large hands

and thick legs. He is quite remark-
able because of his size, and he is a
thorough villain."

People were very surprised at
this. Many of them had heard nothing about it before. Considering the
way the case had been left, it was
felt that Odd had worked hard at it
and scored a lucky success.

Chapter 7

The story goes that Styrmir and Thorarin had a talk together. Styrmir said, "We've been disgraced and humiliated in this case."

Thorarin said that it was what he had expected - "some crafty men must have taken a hand in this."

"Yes," said Styrmir, "but can you see any way of putting it right?"

"I don't think it could be done overnight," said Thorarin.

"What's the best approach?" said Styrmir.

"If we brought a case against them for using bribes in court, then that might stick," said Thorarin.

"That's what we'll do," said Styrmir. Then they set off back to their booths.

They summoned their friends

and kinsmen to a meeting. First there was Hermund Illugason, second Gellir Thorkelsson, third Egil Skulason, fourth Jarnskeggi Einarsson, fifth Skegg-Broddi Bjarnason, sixth Thorgeir Halldoruson, and Styrmir and Thorarin. The eight of them talked together. Styrmir and Thorarin explained the development of the case, and how it stood now, and what a good prospect there was of making a profit from Odd's wealth, and how they would all get rich as a result. Then they made a firm agreement between themselves to back one another up in the case, so that they would be awarded a verdict of outlawry or be given self-judgement. They sealed their partnership with oaths, and were confident that it would not fail, and that no-one would have the daring or intelligence to oppose them. On this note they parted. People rode home from the Assembly, and at first this was kept secret.

Odd was well pleased with his journey to the Assembly, and he and his father got along better now than they had done. Odd had a peaceful winter. During the spring he ran into his father at the baths, and Ofeig asked him the news. Odd said he had heard none, and asked what Ofeig had heard. Ofeig said that Styrmir and Thorarin had gathered some men and were bent on coming to Mel to summon him. Odd asked the reason for this, and Ofeig told him their whole plan.

"I don't think that's a problem," said Odd.

"Maybe it won't be beyond your strength," said Ofeig.

Time passed, and the summoning-days came, and Styrmir and

Thorarin came to Mel with a large following. Odd also had a lot of men there. They announced their case, and summoned Odd to the Assembly on a charge of using illegal bribes in court. Nothing else happened there, and they rode away with their men.

Odd and Ofeig happened to meet again, and they got talking. Ofeig asked him if he still thought it an easy matter.

"I don't think it's a serious case," said Odd.

"That's not the way I see it," said Ofeig. "How much do you know about their preparations?"

Odd said he knew what had happened so far.

"I've a notion that more will follow in its wake," said Ofeig, "because six other leading chieftains have joined forces with them."

"They seem in need of numbers," replied Odd.

"What action will you take now?" asked Ofeig.

"What else but to ride to the Assembly and look for help?" said Odd.

"That seems risky to me, with such a shaky defence," said Ofeig, "and it's a bad idea to stake your honour on having a greater force of men."

"What's to be done then?" said Odd.

"My advice," said Ofeig, "is that during the Assembly you prepare your ship, and be ready to sail with all your movable property before people ride home from the Assembly. Where will your money find the better home, with them when they take it from you, or with me when you give it to me?"

"For you to have it seems a

lesser evil," said Odd.

Then he gave his father a fat purse full of silver, and they parted. Odd prepared his ship and got a crew. The time of the Assembly drew near. These plans went ahead in secret, so that few people knew of them.

Chapter 8

The chieftains rode to the Assembly with a great crowd of men. Old Ofeig was in Styrmir's band. Of the confederates, Egil and Styrmir and Hermund and Thorarin had arranged to meet up on Blaskoga Moor. They all rode south together to the Assembly plain. Skegg-Broddi and Thorgeir Halldoruson from Laugardal rode from the east; Jarnskeggi came from the north, and they met by Reydarmuli. Now all the bands rode down to the plain, and so to the Assembly.

All the talk there was about the case against Odd. Everyone felt sure that nobody would defend it, thinking that few would dare to oppose such powerful chieftains, and that if they did, it would fail. The confederates thought their case as good

68

as won, and bragged a lot about it.
There was no-one with a word to say
against them. Odd had not briefed
anyone to handle the case; as soon as
people had set off for the Assembly,
he started making his ship ready in
Hrutafjord.

One day old Ofeig left his
booth, feeling very uneasy. He could
think of no-one to help him, and
knew it would be hard to put up a
fight. He could see scarcely any
chance of opposing such powerful
chieftains on his own, when there
was no real defence to the charge.
For a long time he wandered about
among the booths, stooping and tottering along, until eventually he
came to the booth of Egil Skulason.
Some men had come there to talk
with Egil. Ofeig walked past and
waited by the door until they went
away. Egil came out with them, and

when he turned round to go back inside, Ofeig stepped up and greeted him. Egil looked him over, and asked who he was.

"My name is Ofeig," he said.

"Are you Odd's father?" asked Egil.

He said that was so.

"Then you'll be wanting to discuss his case, but it's no use talking to me about it, it's gone too far for me to be of any help, and besides, there are others who have more say in it than I do, Styrmir and Thorarin, for example; they're in charge of the case, but we're backing them."

A verse sprang to Ofeig's lips, and he said:

> "Thoughts of my boy
> Were better once,
> Though I never kept
> Odd company;

The fool learned
Little of law,
Though his fists
Were full of cash."
And he went on:
"This old stop-at-home's
Best sport now
Is to mull things over
With men of wisdom.
Don't turn down
A talk with me,
Since people say
You're a sage.

I have other ways of amusing
myself than talking about Odd's affairs. They're not so grand as they
used to be. You won't deny me a
talk with you? It's an old man's
greatest pleasure to while away a
few hours talking to men of your
ilk."
"I won't refuse to talk with

you," said Egil.

Then the two of them went in together and sat down. Ofeig took up the conversation.

"Do you have your own farm, Egil?"

Egil said he had.

"And you live at Borg, don't you?"

"That's right," said Egil.

"I've heard a lot of good and complimentary things about you; they say you keep a generous table and live in fine style. The two of us are not unalike; we both come from good families, and we're free-handed with our goods, yet we're hard-up for money. I've also heard that you like helping your friends."

"I'd be happy to think my reputation was on a par with yours," said Egil, "because I know you're well-born and wise."

"But there is a difference," said Ofeig, "because you are a great chieftain and fear nothing, whatever the obstacle, and you never back down, whoever you're up against, while I am a nobody. But we're pretty much alike in temperament, and it's a great shame that outstanding men like us should be short of money."

"Maybe that's about to change for the better," said Egil.

"How's that?" said Ofeig.

"It seems to me," said Egil, "that if Odd's money comes our way, then the shortage will be over, because we've heard plenty about his wealth."

"It wouldn't be going too far," said Ofeig, "to call him the richest man in Iceland. But you must be curious to know what your share of his wealth would be, since you need it so badly."

"That's true," said Egil, "and you're such a good and wise old chap, you must know all about Odd's wealth."

"I suppose I know more about it than anyone," said Ofeig, "and I can tell you that it's beyond anyone's wildest guess. But I've been working out what your share of it will be."

A verse came to his lips:
"Gold-thirst, gross injustice,
Greed, are what these eight feed on;
 Men's oaths in their mouths
 Mock honour and shock it;
 Heroes of the shields' hard
 Hammering, I damn you;
Share dross, not shining ore,
Shame for the would-be famous."

"That's not likely to happen in a hurry," said Egil, "but you're a good poet."

"I won't put off telling you how much you'll get," said Ofeig, " - one sixteenth of the land at Mel."

"That's outrageous!" said Egil. "Then there's not as much money as I thought. How can that be?"

"You're wrong," said Ofeig, "there's a lot of money, but I reckon that's roughly what you'll get yourself. Didn't you and your confederates all agree that you were to have one half of Odd's wealth, and the men of the Quarter the other half? On that basis I reckon, if there are eight of you, that you'll get half the land at Mel between you, since that's what you must have planned and agreed on. Even though you've gone into this case incredibly rashly, you must have agreed on that much, at least. Or did you by any chance expect that my son Odd would sit tight at home, waiting for you to ride north and fall on him? No!" said Ofeig, "you won't catch Odd napping. Rich he may be, but he's got no less shrewdness and guile when he needs it. And even if you can call him an outlaw, I can't see that stopping the Iceland sea from flowing under the keel of his ship. And when a case has been so unjustly initiated as this one, then the victim can not justly be outlawed, and it will rebound on his prosecutors. And I reckon that by now he'll be at sea with all his goods, apart from the land at Mel - he's leaving that for you. He's heard that it's no great distance from the coast to Borg, once he gets to Borgarfjord. This business will end as it began, so that you'll be shamed and dishonoured in it, and everyone will condemn you, which is what you deserve."

"It's as clear as daylight, now," said Egil, "and it's a tricky case. It was hardly likely that Odd would be caught napping, and I can't blame him for that, because there are some men in this case, the ones stirring it up most, whom I would be pleased to see disgraced, like Styrmir or Thorarin, and Hermund."

"It's going to turn out as they deserve," said Ofeig, "and many men will condemn them for this. But it seems wrong to me that you yourself should come out of it badly, because you're a man after my own heart, and the best one of you confeder- ates."

Then he lowered a fat purse of money from underneath his cloak. Egil followed it with his eyes. Ofeig watched this, and whisked it smartly up under the cloak, and said:

"The way things are, Egil, I expect it will go pretty much as I've told you. Now I'm going to do you a favour."

He untied the purse and poured the silver out on to the hem of Egil's cloak. There were two hundred and forty ounces of the best silver.

"This is what you'll get from me," said Ofeig, "if you don't stand in the way of my defence, and it's your share of the honour."

"What an old rogue you are!" said Egil. "You can't be expecting me to break my oath!"

"You people are not what you think yourselves to be," said Ofeig. "You want to be called chieftains, but you're not so clever when it comes to finding your way out of trouble. You won't have to break your oath, because I'm going to hit on a plan for you to keep it."

"What plan is that?" said Egil.

"Didn't you all agree that you would get a verdict either of outlawry or self-judgement?" asked Ofeig.

Egil said that was so.

"It may well be," said Ofeig, "that we kinsmen of Odd will be allowed to choose which of the two it shall be. Now it might turn out that you will be appointed as arbitrator, in which case I want you to fix the award."

"True enough," said Egil. "You're a crafty old fellow, and a wise one too. But I'm not up to it. I've neither the power nor the men to stand alone against all these chieftains, because if someone thwarts them they'll turn on him viciously."

"How would it be if someone else took your side in the case?" asked Ofeig.

"That would be more like it," said Egil.

"Which one of the confederates would you choose first?" said Ofeig. "Imagine that I could take my pick of them all."

"There are two of them," said Egil. "Hermund is my closest kinsman, but we don't get on together. The other one is Gellir - I'll choose him."

"That's a hard one," said Ofeig, "because apart from you, I wish them all bad luck from this case. But he will have the sense to see which is the better choice - to have money and honour, or to lose the money and be disgraced. But will you agree now to cut down the award if you're appointed as arbitrator?"

"I certainly will," said Egil.

"Then let this be a hard and

fast agreement between us," said
Ofeig, "and I'll be back here to you
in a while."

Chapter 9

Now Ofeig left Egil and went away. He wandered about among the booths, dragging his heels, but not so dejected in his mind as he was tottering of foot, nor with his case as weak as his walk was limping. Eventually he came to Gellir Thorkelsson's booth, and had him called outside. He came out and greeted Ofeig first, since he had humble manners, and asked him his business.

"I was just wandering by," said Ofeig.

"You'll be wanting to talk about Odd's case," said Gellir.

"I don't want to talk about it," said Ofeig, "and as far as I'm concerned, it's out of my hands, and I'll find myself some other sport."

"Then what do you want to talk

about?" said Gellir.

"I've been told you're a wise man," said Ofeig, "and I like talking to wise men."

Then they sat down and got into conversation.

"Which of the young men in the western districts do you think likely to become great chieftains?" asked Ofeig.

Gellir said there was a good choice of such men, and mentioned the sons of Snorri the Priest, and the men of Eyr.

"That's just what I've been told," said Ofeig, "and it's clear that I've come to a good source of information, now that I'm talking with a man who is both truthful and straightforward. But which young women there in the west are the best matches?"

Gellir mentioned the daughters

of Snorri the Priest and the daughters of Steinthor of Eyr.

"That's what I've been told," said Ofeig, "but tell me, don't you have some daughters yourself?"

Gellir said that was a fact.

"Why didn't you mention them?" asked Ofeig. "On the face of things, no daughters could be more beautiful than yours. Are they not married?"

"No," said Gellir.

"Why's that?" said Ofeig.

"Because," said Gellir, "no men who are both wealthy and well-established, with powerful kinsmen and their own high accomplishments, have made proposals. Although I'm not a rich man, I'm still fussy about husbands for them, because of our lineage and honour. But I'm not letting you ask all the questions. Which men up there in the north are likely to be chieftains?"

"There's a good choice," replied Ofeig. First I'd say Einar, Jarnskeggi's son, and then Hall Styrmisson. Some people also say that my son Odd is a promising man. In fact, now we come to the offer he asked me to make you, that he would like to marry into your family, and wed your daughter Ragnhild."

"Yes," said Gellir, "there was a time when that would have found a favourable answer, but the way things are now, I think it's best forgotten."

"What's the reason for that?" said Ofeig.

"The way things are, your son Odd's affairs look pretty murky," said Gellir.

"I'll tell you for a fact," said Ofeig, "that you'll never find a better match. Everyone would agree that he's as accomplished as the best of them; he lacks neither wealth nor good lineage. But you're badly in need of money, and it could well be that you would gain some strength from him, because he's a man who is generously inclined towards his friends."

"It might be looked into," said Gellir, "if this lawsuit were not hanging over him."

"Don't talk of that nonsense!" said Ofeig. "It's of no importance, except for the dishonour and utter ridicule it will bring on all those who are involved in it."

"All the same, there's no less chance of it turning out the other way," said Gellir, "and I won't agree to your offer. But if that obstacle could be removed, then I would be willing."

"It is possible, Gellir," said

Ofeig, "that you will all get rich from this. But I can tell you what your share of it will be, because I know very well, and at the very most you eight confederates will get half the land at Mel. Even then your share will be a paltry one – you'll get a little of the property, but you will have lost the self-reliance and manliness for which you used to be known as one of the best men in the country."

Gellir asked why that might be.

"By now, Odd is probably out at sea with all his possessions, except for the land at Mel," said Ofeig. "You could hardly expect him to sit back and give you lot a free hand with his goods. No!" said Ofeig, "on the other hand, he said that if he came to Breidafjord he would find your farm, and then he could take his pick of your daughters for a wife, and he said he had enough firewood to burn your house down if he felt like it. The same if he came to Borgarford - he had heard it was no long walk from the coast to Borg. He also said he would find Jarnskeggi's farm if he got to Eyjafjord. And the same if he came to the eastern fjords, that he would find out where Skegg-Broddi lives. It doesn't matter to him if he never sees Iceland again, while you will get just what you deserve from all this - shame and disgrace. Now I think it's wrong that a fine chieftain like you used to be should suffer such a blow, and I would like to save you from it."

"You may be right," said Gellir, "and it wouldn't worry me if something went astray with the seizure of the property. I let myself be led into this by my friends rather than feeling really convinced about it in my own mind."

"As soon as there's not so much pressure on you," said Ofeig, "you'll see that there's more honour for you in marrying your daughter to my son Odd, just as I said at first. Look, here's the money he sent you! He said he would pay her dowry himself, because he knows how hard up you are. This is two hundred and forty ounces of the finest silver to be found anywhere. Just think now, who else would offer you a chance like this to marry off your daughter to a man who even pays the dowry himself, and who's never going to leave you in want, while your daughter lands on a fortune!"

"It's a great chance," said Gellir, "and so great that it's hard to decide. But on no account am I going to betray those who trust me, even though this case will bring nothing but mockery and scorn."

"You chieftains are incredibly stupid!" said Ofeig. "Who is urging you to betray those who trusted you, or to go back on your oaths? It may turn out that you will be appointed as arbitrator, and then you can cut down the amount of the award and still keep your oaths."

"That's true," said Gellir. "You're a very crafty old chap, and slippery as an eel! But I can't handle all of them alone."

"How would it be if I got some-one else?" said Ofeig. "Would you help our case then?"

"I would," said Gellir, "if you arrange it so that I'm to arbitrate."

"Which one would you choose to be with you?" asked Ofeig.

"I'll choose Egil," said Gellir.

"He's closest to me."

"What a choice!" said Ofeig, "the worst one of the whole bunch! I'm not at all keen to give him a share of the honour, and I don't know if I'll do it."

"You decide then," said Gellir.

"Will you co-operate if I bring him into it with you?" asked Ofeig. "He's bound to see that it's better to get some honour than none at all."

"Since I stand to gain so much," said Gellir, "then I think I'll risk it."

"Egil and I have already talked it over," said Ofeig, "and he didn't feel it would be too difficult to handle, and he has agreed. Now I'll advise you what to do. You confederates and your followers are always walking about together, so nobody will suspect anything if you and Egil talk as much as you like when you go to evensong."

Gellir took the money, and now it was settled between them.

Ofeig went back to Egil's booth, neither slowly nor crooked, and not hunched up either. He told Egil how things stood. He was satisfied. Later in the evening people went to evensong, and Egil and Gellir talked with each other and arranged things between themselves. No one suspected anything.

Chapter 10

Now it is said that on the following day, men thronged to the Law Rock. Egil and Gellir gathered their friends around them. Ofeig mustered with Styrmir and Thorarin. When everyone who was involved had come to the Law Rock, Ofeig asked for a hearing, and spoke up:

"I have not meddled in my son Odd's case so far, but now I see that we have here the men who are in charge of it. First I want to call on Hermund in this case, which has been initiated with unheard-of irregularity, and pursued in the same way, and that's how it's likely to end. I would like to ask if a settlement can be reached in this case."

"We'll accept nothing but self-judgement," replied Hermund.

"You'll hardly find a precedent for one man granting self-judgement to eight others," said Ofeig, "but there are precedents for one man granting it to one other. Seeing that the case has been conducted more outlandishly than any other, then I would suggest that two of your group should make the judgement."

"We will certainly agree to that," said Hermund, "and we don't mind which two do it."

"Then you would not deny me this shred of dignity," said Ofeig, "to choose two of you confederates personally?"

"Yes, yes," said Hermund.

"Only agree today to what you won't regret tomorrow," said Thorarin.

"There'll be no going back on it," said Hermund.

Then Ofeig looked for men to

stand surety, which was easy since the outlay seemed secure. Then handshakes were exchanged, sealing the sum to be awarded by Ofeig's nominees; the confederates sealed by handshakes the dropping of the charges.

Then it was decided that the confederates should go up to the Assembly plain with their supporters. Gellir's and Egil's groups both went together. They sat down on a certain spot, and formed a ring. Ofeig went into the ring, looked around and lifted the hood of his cloak; he stroked his arms and stood leaning back with his stomach thrust out; his eyes glittered, and then he spoke:

"There you sit, Styrmir! People will think it curious if I don't let you touch a case that I have on hand, since I am one of your followers, and it is to you that I should

look for help, but you have received
many good gifts from me and repaid
them all badly. I recall that you
were the first man to show hostility
to my son Odd in this affair, and
you had most to do with bringing the
case forward. I eliminate you."

"There you sit, Thorarin!" said
Ofeig, "and it certainly isn't true
that you lack the intelligence to
judge this case. But you set out to
harm Odd in this affair, and you
were the first to push the case forward with Styrmir, and for that I
eliminate you."

"There you sit, Hermund, a
great chieftain, and I think the case
would be in good hands if it were
entrusted to you. But no-one has
been as rampant as you since this
thing was started, and it's plain that
you wished to disgrace us publicly.
Nothing but spite and greed drew

you into it, for you're not short of money, and I eliminate you."

"There you sit, Jarnskeggi! and you don't lack the ambition to arbitrate the case, and you wouldn't be vexed if it were put in your hands. Your ambition was also great when you had a banner carried before you at the Vodla Assembly, just like a king, but you won't be king over this case, and I eliminate you."

Then Ofeig looked around and spoke:

"There you sit, Skegg-Broddi! Is it true that when you were staying with King Harald Sigurdarson he said he thought you were the Icelander most fit to be a king?"

"The king often spoke well to me," said Broddi, "but it's not so certain that he meant all he said."

"You'll have to be king over something other than this case," said

Ofeig, "and I eliminate you."

"There you sit, Gellir!" said Ofeig, "and nothing but pure money-lust has drawn you into this case. Yet there's some excuse for that, since you are poor and have many obligations. Now although I think you all deserve disgrace, I can see nothing else for it but that someone must have the honour of judging the case, since there are few left and I'm unwilling to choose those whom I have already rejected. I choose you because you are not already known for injustice.

"There you sit, Thorgeir Halldoruson!" said Ofeig, "and it's well known that no case of any weight has ever come your way, because you are incapable of judgement, and have no more sense of it than an ox or an ass, and I eliminate you."

Then Ofeig looked around, and a

verse came to his lips:
> "It's bad for men
> To abide old age,
> She seizes their
> Sight and wits.
> I've had my pick
> Of prized fellows;
> Now I've wound up
> With the wolf's tail.

And I'm in the same position as the wolves; they eat until they reach the tail without realising it. I have had to choose from among many chieftains, and now all there is left is a man from whom everyone expects mischief; he has proved to be more unjust than any of the others, and doesn't care what he does for money as long as he gets it in the end. But if he has not been honest in this case, he has an excuse, for it has entangled many a man who was previously thought honest, but who has now given up courage and man-liness for dishonesty and greed. No-one would imagine that I am going to choose the man from whom everyone expects mischief, because there is not a more slippery character to be found in your faction, but it must come down to this now, since all the others have been eliminated."

At this Egil grinned, and said, "Once more it is not through the wish of others that honour falls to me. What we must do now, Gellir, is to get up and go aside and talk the case over between us."

So they did, and went away from the spot, and sat down. Then Gellir said, "What shall we say about it?"

"My suggestion," said Egil, "is that we award a small fine. I don't know what else will come of it, but it's not going to make us very popular."

"Won't it be just right if we award thirteen ounces of impure silver?" said Gellir, "since the case was very unjustly fabricated, and the worse they like it the better it will be. But I'm not keen to announce the award, because I expect they will be furious."

"Take your pick," said Egil, "either announce the settlement or else face the challenges."

"I'll choose to announce it," said Gellir.

Then they went to meet the confederates.

"Let's stand up to hear this humiliation," said Hermund.

"We'll get no wiser later on," said Gellir, "and it all comes to one end. The judgement of myself and Egil is that the award to us confederates shall be thirteen ounces of silver."

"Did I hear right," said Hermund. "Did you say thirteen hundred ounces of silver?"

"You didn't stand up so that you could sit on your ear, Hermund," said Egil. "Thirteen ounces, of course, and in money that none but a pauper would take. It's to be paid in brooch-scrapings and ring-fragments and worthless garbage that you'll hate."

"You've betrayed us, Egil," said Hermund.

"Is that so?" said Egil, "do you think you've been betrayed?"

"I think I've been betrayed, and it's you who have betrayed me."

"I'm glad to betray a man who trusts nobody, not even himself, and I've got facts to prove what I'm saying. You buried your money in such a thick fog that you knew you would never find it even if you had a fancy to."

"This is like all your other lies, Egil," said Hermund. "In the winter when you came to my house after I had invited you from your hovel for Christmas, you were glad, as was to be expected. But when Christmas was over you were miserable, as was to be expected, since you did not fancy going home to starve. When I saw that, then I invited you and one of your men to stay with me, and you accepted gladly. But in the spring, after Easter, when you got home to Borg, you said that thirty of my old horses that had been feeding themselves out in the snow had died and all had been eaten at my table."

"Since it's impossible to exaggerate your stinginess," said Egil, "I would think few or none of them were actually eaten. But everyone knows that I and my men never lack food, even though I'm not so well off, but your household affairs are the sort you should keep quiet about."

"I would hope," said Hermund, "that the two of us are not both at the Assembly next summer!"

"Now I'll say something I thought I would never say," said Egil, "and I bless you for having spoken, because it has been prophesied that I will die of old age, and I'll be well pleased if the trolls take you first."

Then Styrmir said, "Those who speak worst about you, Egil, and call you a swindler, speak truest."

"Well, that's fine," said Egil. "The more you insult me, and the more truth you find in it, then the better I like it, since I've been told that one of your drunken amusements

is to compare men, and you compare
yourself to me. And it's sure that
there's some evil in you which others know nothing of, but you must
know your own character best. But
in one thing we are different - we
each pledge to help the other, and I
support you as far as I am able, and
hold nothing back, but you take to
your heels as soon as the black-
handled battle-axes start flying.
And it's also true that although my
household is not prosperous, no-one
gets refused a meal; but you are
stingy with your victuals, and the
proof of it is that you've got a bowl
called "Food-Lucky," and no-one who
comes to your house knows what's in
it, apart from you. It's only right
that my household should have little
to eat when times are hard, but
hardly right for a man to starve his
household when there's plenty of

food.   Just guess who I'm talking about!"

Styrmir went quiet.

Then Thorarin stood up.

"Shut up and sit down, Thorarin," said Egil, "and don't interrupt, or I'll insult you so much you'll wish you had held your tongue. It's no joke, the way you sit there thin as a rake, rubbing your thighs together.   Your servants always laugh about it though."

"Accept good advice, whatever the source," said Thorarin.   He sat down and kept quiet.

Then Thorgeir said, "Everyone can see that an award of only thirteen ounces of silver for so serious an indictment is a meaningless and stupid judgement."

"But I thought you would have found it a meaningful award," said Egil, "and so you will if you think it

106

over, for then you'll remember the
autumn Assembly at Rang River,
when that old peasant raised thirteen
bumps on your head, and you took
thirteen ewes with their lambs from
him as compensation. I thought this
reminder would be just what you
wanted."

Thorgeir said nothing. Skegg-
Broddi and Jarnskeggi had no desire
to bandy words with Egil.

Then Ofeig said, "Now I will
speak you a verse, so that this Assembly and the outcome of this case
may be better remembered:
> For less than this matter
> Most other men would boast;
> My poem will proclaim
> Me pleased, my pain now eased.
> A wretch, lacking riches,
> Rags round their eyes I wound
> To hoodwink proud headmen,
> Hurled sand in surly faces."

Egil said, "You may well boast about it, since no one man has ever taken more wind out of so many chieftains' sails."

After that people went back to their booths. Gellir said to Egil, "I want us both to stick together with all our men."

They did so. For the rest of the Assembly there was much muttering of threats, and the confederates were furious about the result of the case. No-one wanted the money, and it hung around the Assembly field. Then everyone rode home from the Assembly.

Chapter 11

When the father and son met,
Odd was ready to put to sea. Ofeig
told Odd that he had given them
self-judgement.

"You abandoned the case like a
wretch," said Odd.

"Even so, it wasn't a complete
disaster, son," said Ofeig, and told
Odd all the details, and that he was
betrothed. Then Odd thanked him
for his help, and felt that Ofeig had
done far more that he had thought
possible. He told him that he would
never go short of money.

"Now you must put to sea, as
you planned," said Ofeig, "but your
wedding will be at Mel six weeks
before summer ends."

After that, father and son parted
in love and friendship. Odd set
sail, and got a wind which took him

north to Thorgeirsfjord. Some Nor-
wegian merchants were already lying
there. Then the wind died, and they
stayed there several nights. Odd
thought the wind was too slow in
getting up, so he climbed a high fell,
and saw that outside the fjord the
wind was in a different quarter. He
returned to the ship, and told the
crew to row out of the fjord. The
Norwegians made fun of them, and
said it would be a long row to Nor-
way.

"Who knows you won't still be
here when we return," said Odd.

As soon as they got out of the
fjord they found a favourable wind,
and didn't strike sail until they
reached the Orkneys. Odd bought
malt and grain there, and stayed a
while making the ship ready. No
sooner had he finished, than an east
wind blew up and they set sail.

They had a good voyage, and when they reached Thorgeirsfjord the merchants were still there. Odd sailed west along the coast and came to Midfjord. He had been away for seven weeks.

Preparations for the wedding feast were made, and there was no lack of fine provisions. A great crowd came, including Gellir and Egil and many other prominent men. The feast went splendidly; people said that no better wedding had ever been held in the whole country. When the feast came to an end, everyone was sent on their way with fine gifts, the most lavish going to Gellir.

Gellir said to Odd, "I would like Egil to be treated well, for he deserves it."

"I would think my father has treated him well already," said

111

Odd.

"Go one better," said Gellir. Then he and his men rode off.

When Egil set out, Odd saw him on his way and thanked him for his help.

"I can never do as well by you as I ought," said Odd, "but yesterday I had sixty wethers and two oxen driven south to Borg, and they'll be waiting at home for you. I'll never treat you anything but well, as long as we both live."

Egil was delighted. They confirmed their friendship, and then parted. Egil went home to Borg.

Chapter 12

That same autumn, Hermund gathered forces and went out to the Assembly at Hvamm, intending to go to Borg and burn Egil in his house. When they came out by Valfell, they heard what sounded like a bowstring twang up on the fell, and suddenly Hermund felt ill, and had a stinging pain under his arm, and they had to turn back. The sickness grew worse, and when they came to Thorgautsstadir they had to lift him off his horse. They sent to Sidumuli for a priest. By the time he came, Hermund was unable to speak, and the priest stayed by him. Once when the priest was bending over him, his lips murmured, "Two hundreds in the ghyll, two hundreds in the ghyll." Then he died, and his life ended just as is said here.

Odd remained on his farm in great splendour and got on well with his wife.

All this time nothing had been heard of Ospak. A man called Mar Hildisson married Svala and took over the farm at Svolustadir. He had a brother called Bjalfi, a half-wit, but a strong man. There was a man called Bergthor, who lived at Bodvarsholar. He had summed up the case in which Ospak was outlawed.

One evening at Bodvarsholar, when men were sitting round the fire, a man came to the door and asked the farmer to step outside. He realised it was Ospak who had come, and refused. Ospak kept on urging him out, but for all that he didn't go, and forbade his men to go either. That's how the meeting ended, but in the morning, when the women went

to the byre, nine of the cows were fatally wounded.

This news spread far and wide. Later, as time passed by, a man happened to arrive at Svolustadir. He went into the room where Mar was sleeping. It was early in the morning. The man went up to the bed and thrust at Mar with a short sword, wounding him in the belly. It was Ospak. He spoke a verse:

"From the sheath I drew
The sword new-sharpened;
Into the guts of Mar
I made it slide.
I could not suffer
The son of Hildir
Lying in the arms
Of lovely Svala."

Just as he was turning to the door, Bjalfi jumped up and stabbed him with a whittling knife. Ospak went to a farm called Borgarhol and announced the killing there. Then he went away, and nothing was heard of him for a while. The news of Mar's killing got about and was condemned.

Then it happened that Odd's best stud-horses, five of them, were all found dead; people blamed Ospak for this. In the autumn when men went to round up the sheep, they found a cave in the cliff. Inside there was a dead man, and next to him was a basin full of blood, and it was black as pitch. It was Ospak. People thought that the wound Bjalfi gave him must have been serious, and that he had died from starvation. That was the end of Ospak. There is no record of any prosecution being brought for the killing of Mar or Ospak.

Odd lived at Mel until old age, and was considered a very prominent

Ospak's body found in a cave.

119

man. The men of Midfjord are descended from him, like Snorri Kalfsson and many other great men. Odd and Ofeig always kept up their kinship and friendship after these events. And there is where the story ends.

Also published by Llanerch:

BEOWULF translated by John Porter, with drawings by Nicholas Parry.

THE LIFE AND DEATH OF CORMAC THE SCALD (KORMAC'S SAGA) translated from the Icelandic; Collingwood and Stefansson. Illustrated facsimile.

SCANDINAVIAN BRITAIN by W. G. Collingwood; facsimile.

A HANDBOOK OF THE OLD NORTHERN RUNIC MONUMENTS OF SCANDINAVIA AND ENGLAND by G. Stephens; small-paper reprint; illus.

For a complete list of small-press editions and facsimile reprints on ancient history/legend/folk-lore etc., write to Llanerch Publishers, Felinfach, Lampeter, Dyfed. SA488PJ.

122